D1143404

for Alan & Colin

Phaidon Press Limited
Regent's Wharf
All Saints Street
London N1 9PA

Phaidon Press Inc.
180 Varick Street
New York, NY 10014

www.phaidon.com

This edition © 2008 Phaidon Press Limited
First published in 1962 by Anthony Blond Limited

ISBN 978 0 7148 4850 1 (UK/US edition)

A CIP catalogue record for this book
is available from the British Library.

Designed by Bob Gill
Jacket photograph by Rod Munro
Printed in China

What
Colour
Is Your
World?
by
Bob Gill

Britain and the United States are two very different countries.
One has a Queen, the other a President. One is an island,
the other is not. However, there is one thing that the people
who live in these two countries do have in common: they both
speak the same language, English. But, have you ever noticed
how differently we say things? *Tomato* is one of the most
famous examples! Sometimes we even spell the same word in
a different way. If you look at the cover of this book, you'll see
that the word 'colour' is spelt the British way, with a 'u'.
But on this page, it's spelt the American way, without a 'u'.
Neither is wrong nor right. They are just different ways of
doing the same thing. In Australia and Canada colour is spelt
the same way as in Britain.

What color*
is the world?

Suppose you
asked a gardener?
"Simple!" he would
say, "My world is

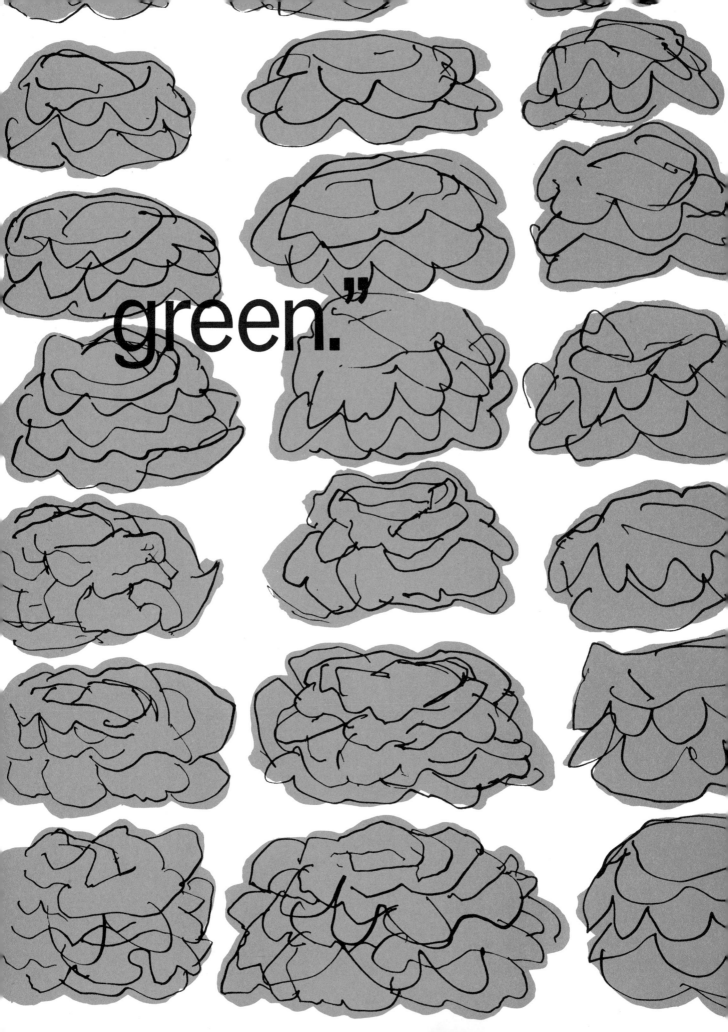

green."

Suppose
you asked a
beachcomber?
"Easy!"
he would say,
"My world is

yellow."

Suppose
you asked
a colonel?
"Attention!"
he would
say, "My
world is
brown."

Suppose bricklayer ? would say,

you asked a
"Clunk!" he
"My world is red."

Suppose
you asked
a milkman?
"Here!" he
would say,
"My world

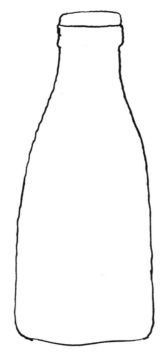

is white."

Suppose you asked a king? "Humph!" he would say, "My world is purple."

Y

Suppose you asked a diver? "Glub!" he would say, "My world is blue."

Suppose
you asked a
stargazer?
"Look!"
he would say,
"My world is
black."

But suppose you asked an artist? "It's hard to tell," he would answer. "Colours keep changing. Look at this... In my world kings may be

green

or
shells
purple

or bricks

grey and black.

And if I feel like it, I can make the sky yellow

or the
ocean
orange

or milk
brown or
soldiers
white

or cabbage blue"

My world is
whatever colour
I wish.

How do you feel?
What colour
is your world?